CAS ... NO
SHADOW

Best Wishes

David

DAVID BRETT SAUNDERS

Books by David Brett Saunders

ROMANS & BRITONS
For Honour And Not For Glory

VIKINGS & SAXONS
All Sins Must Be Paid For

LATER MIDDLE AGES
Cast No Shadow

HIGH MIDDLE AGES
Awful The Many Foul Deeds

Copyright © 2021 David Brett Saunders

Designed by Jeremy Paxton

Set in 11pt Palatino Linotype

Printed in the UK

All rights reserved

1 4 6 8 10 12 14 16 18

ISBN: 978-0-9567753-6-8

List of Contents

---

*Dedicated to my wife Bev
and my lovely daughters
Emma, Claire and Amy*

*Also a special mention to the much longer
and much better written novels of
Sharon Penman set in Medieval times*

*And in fond remembrance of all the
wonderful books of Rosemary Sutcliff*

A Literary Quote

"I have trod the upward
and the downward slope;
I have endured
and done in days before;
I have longed for all,
and bid farewell to hope;
And I have lived and loved,
and closed the door."

from Songs Of Travel
written by Robert Louis Stevenson (1850-1894)

Author's Note

If this all seems too much like a regurgitated history lesson then I am very sorry; but every day makes its own piece of history somewhere and we are all living through these eventful times.

List of Fictional Characters

MARGOT
formerly called Marguerite

JEAN DE SAVIGNAC
soldier and swordsman for hire

TOM BUCKLE
young scamp and pickpocket

GWYN THE INNKEEPER
Welsh tavern keeper in Gloucester

GILLES DE BOUTON
follower of Simon de Montfort

List of Historical Characters

HENRY PLANTAGENET
born 1st October 1207 – died 16th November 1272
son of King John and became
King Henry III of England 1216 – 1272

PRINCE EDWARD
born 18th June 1239 – died 7th July 1307
became King Edward I of England 1272 – 1307
Also known as Edward Longshanks due to his height
and as the conqueror of Wales and the Hammer of the Scots

SIMON DE MONTFORT
born c. 1208 – died 4th August 1265
6th Earl of Leicester and married in 1238 to Princess Eleanor

ELEANOR DE MONTFORT
born 1215 – died 13th April 1275
Also known as Eleanor of England and Countess of Leicester
daughter of King John and sister of King Henry III

SIMON THE YOUNGER
born April 1240 – died 1271
Second son of Simon and Eleanor de Montfort

GILBERT DE CLARE
born 2nd September 1243 – died 7th December 1295
7th Earl of Gloucester
and also known as Red Gilbert or the Red Earl

Statement

Good or bad; right or wrong; saint or sinner – It's easy to say you can make the distinctions between, but we all walk along a very fine line – sometimes on firm ground; sometimes close to the edge.

You might look on in shock and abhorrence at the duplicity that occurred, but times were different then and you had to shift for yourself to make your way.

You may even ask yourself: How is she supposed to live with what she has done? Was she made bitter and twisted by grief and hate? Blinded by the need to rid herself of it all?

And the search for true release through revenge is like an elusive chase for the mythical unicorn.

You might call her an evil plotter involved in causing many deaths, who lost her way in pursuing a desperate need for revenge. But you would be wrong to presume to sit in judgement over her –

She knew what she was doing and that it could be seen as wrong, but it felt right to her and the only true course of action – and she did not regret most of what she did!

Prologue

Margot is the heroine of this tale but that was not the name she was born with. Her given name was Marguerite, which is derived from the Ancient Greek word for pearl.

Marguerite grew up in a small village in Gascony which was an old province of southwestern France, vaguely defined but broadly South and East of Bordeaux.

The name Gascony comes from the same root as the word Basque, and the Gascon language spoken then in the Middle Ages appeared to be similar to a variant of Basque.

The Duchy of Gascony became part of England's vast possessions throughout France in 1152 after the marriage of the famed Eleanor of Aquitaine to the future King Henry II.

In 1248 Simon de Montfort, the French born 6th Earl of Leicester and then a royal favourite, was appointed Governor of the unsettled Duchy of Gascony by the current King Henry III.

And bad things happen in sunshine as well as in shadows……

Chapter 1 – 1250

Twelve year old Marguerite could hear raised voices coming from the courtyard of their manor house in the little village of Seissan. Sauntering over she could see a tall young man remonstrating with her gruff grey-haired father.

"My uncle said to tell you to steer clear of getting involved with those Seigneurs of Auch who are now in revolt against the Governor."

"Why you young pup! How dare you tell me what to do!" thundered the red-faced old man.

"I was not telling you what to do, sir, just passing on the message from my uncle" spluttered the by now equally red-faced younger man, though made so by nervous embarrassment rather than by anger.

Looking at him Marguerite noticed that he was quite pleasant looking though his left earlobe was missing.

"My uncle just says that the Governor has too many soldiers at his disposal and will eventually succeed in beating off any Gascon attempts at trying to resist his many recent unjust laws."

"It seems your uncle has a lot to say, young man, and I dare say much of it is sound advice; but I have relatives in Auch and I feel obligated to join them in fighting against the vile abuses of this Earl Simon de Montfort. Hopefully we can beat him and reverse these harsh impositions on all us Gascons."

"My uncle says we should just bypass him and appeal directly to King Henry in England to seek restitution."

"Well as Earl Simon is a favourite of the king and married to his sister I do not think that will be much use currently. Still I appreciate your riding over to tell me the latest news. Stay and take a cup of wine with me."

"Thank you for your kind offer but I must decline; I have to ride on over to your neighbour to pass on the news to him."

With that he got back on his horse and turned it out of the courtyard. As he rode off he looked down at Marguerite and smiled at her.

Chapter 2 – 1251

The next few months did not go well for the Gascon rebels; the young man's uncle had been proved right as they were gradually beaten and overwhelmed by the Governor's many brutal soldiers.

Marguerite's father had been involved in a few local skirmishes but then came back home later on looking tired, older and dejected.

After a dry and sunny summer the manor's farmers and people were just getting the last of the plentiful wheat harvest in when suddenly out of the North came a large group of armed horsemen.

They attacked the defenceless men and women working in the fields and viciously killed and slew them.

The lord of the manor came out of the house buckling on his trusty sword belt and with a few other men tried to fight back but all to no avail.

The old man was surrounded by several soldiers and was slain by a spear thrust to the chest.

Then the raiders plundered the harvested grain in stolen carts and finally set fire to the barns and buildings of the manor complex before they rode off.

Marguerite was on the way back from running an errand for her mother down at the distant mill when she first saw the thick black smoke rising into the air.

She picked up her skirts and ran towards the manor house from where the smoke was climbing thickest.

She came upon a harrowing scene of death and destruction – flaming buildings and dead people lying everywhere.

Appalled she saw her dead mother and little brother lying outside the burning house, and then over near the barns her bloodstained father's lifeless corpse with many gory wounds.

Just then she heard loud hoofbeats and looked up to see a lone horseman riding furiously towards the raging inferno of the manor.

Frightened she wondered where she could run away to – but surely not anywhere safe in the time available.

Transfixed and not moving, she slowly realised the rider was that young man she had seen last year.

He pulled up in a flurry of dust and ashes and jumped down to the ground and ran towards her. Marguerite was silent and in shock.

"I was coming to warn you all but I see I am too late. Oh my God, what a disaster – all these dead bodies! I am so sorry."

He seemed distraught but then tried to pull himself together.

"My name is Jean and I know your name is Marguerite. Come on, you cannot stay here; nothing is left and you are not safe. I must take you away from here. We will go to my uncle's estate at Savignac and he can say what to do next."

Marguerite vaguely nodded her head and allowed the young man to take her hand and lead her towards his horse and then lift her up to sit in front of him.

As they rode away Marguerite, eyes filled with welling tears, looked back one final time at the blackened ruins of what had once been her family home. Totally destroyed and all her family dead now.

Chapter 3 – 1251 to 1252

After a couple of days in Savignac, Jean's uncle sent word to Marguerite's father's relations in Auch asking if they would take the girl in.

Her relatives were happy to do so and accordingly Jean and a couple of loyal armed men escorted her northwards towards what was the small provincial capital of Gascony.

Marguerite did not say very much on the journey but she appreciated Jean's quiet support and courteous manner.

Once in the busy town of Auch and safely dropped off at her relatives Jean de Savignac bade his farewells and wished her well. Marguerite thanked him back demurely.

There had been little time to lament, to mourn, to grieve.

Over the following months Marguerite's cousins looked after her well and compassionately; and although sometimes she still cried herself to sleep, gradually the flow of tears dried up slightly and a strong-willed resolve built up in Marguerite.

Early on in 1252 the prominent Gascon Seigneurs, merchants and worthies agreed upon the idea of sending a group of Gascon leaders over to London to see King Henry III and ask for him to curb the Governor's powers and seek restitution for their losses.

They decided to bring Marguerite over to England with them to show her off as the sole survivor of an atrocious attack on a little Gascon village.

Marguerite was not really at all sure about wanting to be made to do this, but felt she wanted to show some support for her fellow Gascons' cause.

Her relations gave her some new clothes to take and as well a purse full of money that her late father had kept separately in Auch; and importantly also a letter of introduction to some people in England's capital of London.

They wished her adieu and she was part of the group that later left Auch by horse and cart to travel the long distance to the major regional town and harbour of Bordeaux in the western part of Aquitaine.

The men of the party were well armed and alert as they did not want to be open to attack by any of the Governor's men who might seek to stop them from heading overseas.

Shortly thereafter they reached the bustling town of Bordeaux from where they took ship over to England.

Chapter 4 – 1252

The Gascons landed at the port of London and were housed in various places near the Old Jewry, the location of many of the Jews living in London.

There were connections between the Gascons and the London Jews as they had loaned the money to make the trip to London possible.

The Gascon leaders appealed to King Henry III and their bitter complaints forced the king to listen to the outcry and institute a formal inquiry into Earl Simon's actions and administration in the Duchy of Gascony.

In May 1252 Simon de Montfort was recalled to London, and King Henry threatened to put him on trial for mismanagement, but Earl Simon angrily reminded the king that he could not be sacked in such manner.

When King Henry replied that he was not bound by an oath made to a traitor, hot-headed Simon roared back "Were thou not my king it would be an ill hour for you!"

Earl Simon was eventually formally acquitted on the charges of oppression of the Gascons, but his accounts were disputed by King Henry and in high dudgeon Simon de Montfort left for his estates in France.

Some success for the Gascons maybe, but no further adequate restitution was made for their losses and the Gascon leaders set out to return home.

However it wasn't deemed safe for Marguerite to return as she did not really have a home anymore and she might still be subject to attack by men connected to the Earl.

She and her letter of introduction were presented to Elyas of London, the leader of the Jewish community in the capital. Due to his past dealings with her relatives he was happy to take on responsibility for Marguerite's welfare and upbringing.

Elyas was very understanding and supportive of her difficult position.

"Perhaps it might be better to change your name to provide you with some anonymity and give protection from further recognition. We shall call you Margot, which name is derived from the pearl and its purity."

And Margot, as she now was known, settled in very well with the close-knit Jewish family.

Chapter 5 – 1253 to 1255

Still in 1253 Simon de Montfort was reconciled with his king, following exhortations of the dying Robert Grosseteste, then Bishop of Lincoln and a friend and associate of his.

But the good relations between the fractious Earl and the unreliable king did not last long and they soon fell out again.

King Henry III was oftentimes an unpopular monarch due to his autocratic style, displays of favouritism, bad decisions and his failure to successfully negotiate with his tetchy barons.

In 1254 when a Parliament was summoned in London, for the first time including some elected representatives, Simon sided with the opposition and was one of the leading lights in getting Parliament to refuse to grant a subsidy of further monies to the king.

Meanwhile Margot continued her upbringing and got very friendly with a Jewish girl called Belaset, the daughter of Benedict son of Moses of London.

Thus in 1255 Margot was part of a large group of Jews who went up to Lincoln to celebrate Belaset's upcoming wedding there.

But calamity was about to ensue!

Chapter 6 – 1255

Now it should be stated that it is a strange thing what prejudice and resentment can do to the minds of many people, and throughout history there has been massive prejudice and great harm done to the Jews.

The issue of usury was a large reason for disagreement and it was a practice looked down on by Christians.

Usury is the act of lending money at an interest rate that is considered high or higher than the rate generally permitted by the common rules.

The Jewish moneylenders kept good financial records of the loans given and the corresponding debt bonds.

But if you were a nobleman and needed money to build a castle or a new manor house then where would you get the money from?

Why from a loan taken out from some wealthy Jews of course.

And then you would grumble about the amounts you had to repay and you would say it was all the fault of the Jewish moneylenders!

Gradually King Henry III also taxed the Jews more harshly to help pay for the needs of his Royal Treasury.

This in turn forced Jewish moneylenders to ensure their debts were being paid up or to sell on their debt bonds to others.

Henry's relatives and courtiers in particular would buy up debt bonds, with the express intention of dispossessing the debtors of their lands, which would be forfeit on non-repayment of the loans.

These actions helped to cause further resentment against the Jewish population, and also fuelled later discord of the barons with the king.

Church pronouncements also brought in further restrictions on the activities of the Jews in England in the 1250's.

As well the Pope demanded that Jews lived and were kept separate from Christians, that Christians should not work for Jews (especially in their homes) and that Jews wear badges to identify themselves.

A number of English towns responded by expelling their own local Jewish populations, echoing the previous expulsion of Jews from Leicester orchestrated by Simon de Montfort himself in the past.

Chapter 7 – 1255 to 1256

Whilst up in Lincoln for the wedding celebrations Margot started to hear accusations being made against the Jews regarding the disappearance of a local nine year old boy called Hugh.

Eventually his body was discovered in a well on 29th August 1255 and in a perverse campaign false claims were made of 'blood libel' murder – basically gruesome deaths of children being maliciously and spuriously portrayed as evil Jewish sacrifices.

But the singularly strange case of 'Little Saint Hugh of Lincoln' as it became known was subject to the base acts and abuses of the local people, the Church and the king also.

At the time of these murder accusations, King Henry III had just sold off his rights to tax the Jews to his brother, Richard Earl of Cornwall.

But having lost this source of income, King Henry declared that if a Jew was convicted of any serious crime then any money he had would become forfeit to the Crown.

And furthermore it is likely that the Bishop and Dean of Lincoln steered events to generate the myth of a holy martyr in order to establish a profitable flow of pilgrims to the new shrine at the Cathedral in honour of the dead boy.

Anyway they got a Jew called Copin to confess to the murder, supposedly after being offered some sort of immunity from sentencing in return for his confession.

More likely Copin appears to have been interrogated under torture by John of Lexington, who was the brother of Henry of Lexington the recently new Bishop of Lincoln and also a servant of the king.

Further events exacerbated the strangeness of the handling of this case. King Henry III arrived in Lincoln around a month after the initial arrest and confession.

He ordered Copin to be executed immediately and for ninety prominent Jews to be arrested in connection with Hugh's death and held in the Tower of London. They were to be charged with the crime of ritual murder.

Then eighteen of these Jews were hanged shortly thereafter for refusing to participate in the proceedings by not throwing themselves on the mercy of a Christian jury.

Henry's intervention meant it was the first time an English court had handed out a death sentence for a charge of ritual murder.

King Henry also profited from their deaths as he was entitled to the confiscated property of the convicted Jews.

Garcias Martini, a Knight from Toledo in Spain, was able to intercede for the release of the bride's father Benedict son of Moses of London, and in January 1256 another Christian Jew called John was released.

A trial took place on 03rd February 1256 and the remaining seventy prisoners were condemned to death.

However finally doubts about the fairness of the proceedings were now circulating, and the Dominican monks together with Richard of Cornwall interceded with the king and got him to question the wisdom of pursuing the sentences.

Eventually in May 1256 the remaining prisoners were all released.

Back in her Jewish London home Margot commiserated with and consoled old Elyas whose son had been one of the eighteen Jews hanged.

But Elyas was a broken man, and filled with misery he died soon after himself.

Margot vowed to see the injustice of this whole affair addressed and she was not going to forget it.

Elyas left Margot a substantial amount of money and she was able to use it to look to setting herself up somewhere else further away.

Chapter 8 – 1257

So in 1257 Margot moved westwards to the town of Gloucester and bought herself a fine house in the centre. Gloucester was a long way from the capital of London but was a centre of power and long known as a hotbed of intrigue.

Although still only aged nineteen years old now, Margot had seen many hard times and possessed a maturity far beyond her years.

After some initial whisperings about her situation the townspeople soon got used to her presence.

Margot took on a cook and a young maidservant and settled into the well-appointed wooden timbered house.

She was a couple of doors down from a fine hostelry which was run by an old Welshman called Gwyn; he seemed fine company and in several talks with him outside his inn Margot warmed to him.

She did not frequent the inn as such herself but got her maid to bring over jugs of their finest ale to drink; ale often being safer to drink than water.

The atmosphere in the country did not seem right at all and the summer of 1257 brought a second successive poor grain harvest which produced food shortages.

She was not far from the imposing castle in Gloucester which was the seat of power of the Earls of Gloucester.

The current 6th Earl was Richard de Clare aged in his mid-thirties and a powerful baron of the realm and a close associate of Simon de Montfort.

He had a fourteen year old red-headed son called Gilbert who was already espoused to an older woman Alice de Lusignan who was a half-niece to King Henry III.

Margot judiciously made enquiries about the Earl of Gloucester with Gwyn and gradually found out that he was not a great supporter of any friend of Simon de Montfort.

Cautiously and discreetly Margot suggested that she also was not taken with the bold charisma of Earl Simon as well, and thus got herself into Gwyn's good favour.

Gwyn seemed pleased to confide in Margot and told her some interesting things about his youthful past in Wales, and about how many years ago in the Welsh Marches border region a couple of his brothers had been killed in fighting against Simon de Montfort's men.

Margot finally told him that she had some old scores to settle too.

Chapter 9 – 1258

In early 1258 Simon de Montfort and his family visited Gloucester Castle to allow him to meet up with Richard de Clare and discuss the important matters of the realm and their opposition to the purposeless and arbitrary actions of the king.

And this is what led to Margot coming into contact with the orbit of the de Montfort family.

She and her maid had just been out to buy some fabrics to make dresses with when they came upon Eleanor de Montfort and her young six year old daughter also called Eleanor.

The young girl had fallen over and was about to start crying when Margot reached down and gave her a piece of fabric to hold and picked her up off the ground.

Eleanor de Montfort, who was a sister to the king and a princess in her own right, smiled and thanked Margot and asked her to walk with them.

Margot turned to her maidservant and told her to go back home with the fabrics.

The Lady Eleanor asked who she was and Margot took the opportunity to spin her this tale: "I am Margot de Belvoir the orphaned daughter of a lord displaced from France and now living here in Gloucester."

"Oh how interesting and how charming you are. The Earl of Gloucester is giving a banquet for us tonight at the castle; would you like to come as my special guest?"

"Why most certainly, my Lady, I should be delighted."

And so after saying their goodbyes Margot hurried back home and put on her finest velvet dress and richest looking cloak.

Later she walked up to the castle in the early Spring evening and was soon after ushered into the Great Hall blazing with the light of many candles and a massive roaring log fire.

Chapter 10 – 1258

Margot was introduced by the Lady Eleanor to her husband the famed Simon de Montfort and the Earl of Gloucester.

Margot explained that she was a fairly recent arrival to the town of Gloucester having come from France via London. Her courtly French manners went down well with the nobles and she was accepted readily.

Margot found it strange to actually see the Earl Simon up close in the flesh. She noticed that he was a vigorous looking man of about fifty years of age, bright of eye and loud of speech with a certain arrogance in his manner.

When they sat down to eat Margot noticed that there were three seats near her left unfilled.

Just then there was some loud hallooing and shouting and in ran three laughing young men.

They sat down and started to eat and drink with gusto.

Simon de Montfort banged his fist on the heavy table and shouted "Why you young rascals; where are your manners, Henry and Simon, eh?"

"Pardon father, we did not realise the time" said the slightly older of the two.

"Sorry mother" said the younger man, who also looked across at Margot.

"You should be apologising to your host the Earl of Gloucester" said their mother Princess Eleanor.

"And you Jean should surely know better than to get carried away with my mischievous sons" said Earl Simon.

"Sorry my Lord" said the fair-haired man next to Margot who turned slightly, and in doing so she saw that the earlobe of his left ear was missing.

Margot gasped and the man looked at her with keen interest. Margot's heart beat faster. She recognised Jean from years before and she did not want him to mention her real name and forebears.

"I am Margot de Belvoir from Northern France recently arrived here in Gloucester; who are you and where are you from?"

"Oh, well then, I am Jean de Savignac from the Duchy of Gascony and a loyal soldier in the employ of Earl Simon. A pleasure to meet you, my lady" said the older man with a smile playing at the side of his mouth.

Simon de Montfort looked on with some slight curiosity but then went back to his interrupted conversation with Earl Richard.

Another knight from the Earl of Gloucester's retinue, Gilles de Bouton, looked on with barely concealed disdain.

"Oh how pleasant you manners are, bold Jean. But whilst we are in the throes of all this turmoil it seems to me that affairs of the heart matter less. And in these times a woman should mostly be neither seen nor heard to cause distractions. She should cast no shadow to block the light of the great men of state."

Margot went red with embarrassment and anger but kept silent and ignored the ill-mannered and unpleasant man.

Jean also held back on his temper and just said "Each to his own way, Gilles."

The rest of the lengthy banquet passed in a whirl for Margot, and occasionally out of the corner of her eye she saw Jean looking at her thoughtfully.

Finally the meal came to an end and Margot made her excuses and gave her thanks to her hosts.

As she got up to go Jean de Savignac rose also and said forcefully "My lady, I will escort you into town as I would not wish you to come to any harm. Please accept my protection."

"Thank you, that will be most kind of you."

Chapter 11 – 1258

They walked to the castle entrance without saying any words and then as they passed outside Jean let out a long sigh.

"Well, well, this is a strange turn-up for the books then. How are you Marguerite and what is going on?"

"My name is Margot now and it's complicated."

"How so and what are you playing at?"

"And may I ask what are you doing here working for Earl Simon?"

"It's probably complicated too. Look we'd better try and trust each other and tell the truth about how things are."

"How do I know I can trust you?"

"I didn't say anything back there in the hall."

"True."

"I am still the same man that took you away to safety after the death of your family. You can trust me as a fellow Gascon – even if you are no longer claiming to be one anymore!"

"Look, I have been through difficult times since we last met."

"Yes, seven years ago as I recall" said Jean.

"I thank you for saving my life back then and I also have never forgotten" replied Margot.

"Well, what is going on with you?"

"I just have had to take on a different persona and stay out of trouble's plain sight. Why are you working for the Earl who crushed our homeland's brave revolt and got so many Gascons killed?"

31

"Seven years is a long time to get by with little money. My uncle's estate was also later attacked and burnt down. He died thereafter and left me nothing but a little land encumbered with debts."

"So why are you with the Earl – are you true to him or are you playing him false and plotting against him?"

"That's a big question to ask, isn't it?"

"You said to put our cards on the table."

"Yes I did, and what about you then?"

"I want your assurances that you will keep quiet and not breathe a word about this to anyone."

"You have my word of honour as a true Gascon" he said.

"Then I am still out to get revenge for my dead family, all the other dead Gascons and my persecuted friends within the Jews from this damned Earl."

"Oh well indeed, this is the pretty potent stuff of hatred. And I also am not quite all that I appear to be – for although I may now take the Earl's money I may be biding my time listening in on all his plans and waiting for my chance to bring him down. It may take time but I am minded to wait."

"So revenge is driving us both on."

"Yes, but the quest has to be kept well-concealed from prying eyes, before the hope for any ultimate success."

"Then are we agreed to work together to bring him down?"

"Yes Margot, we are."

"How should we go about furthering our aims?"

"I suggest you get more in favour with the Lady Eleanor and see if you can get included in the family circle. I believe the Earls are both heading to Oxford soon for a summons of Parliament. I am departing tomorrow along with his sons."

"I have a good friend here in Gwyn the Innkeeper."

"Then could he become a keeper of messages also?"

"I will have a word with him and see about that" said Margot.

"Good, then we are bound together on this course of action."

"For better or for worse until the bitter end."

Jean left her at her door and retraced his steps back to the castle.

From the corner of a nearby house the shadow of a man looked on questioningly.

Chapter 12 – 1258

Margot became friendlier with Princess Eleanor and became part of her circle of ladies.

Meanwhile in June 1258 Simon de Montfort and Richard de Clare went to Oxford for another meeting of Parliament.

King Henry was in dire financial straits as he had unwisely pledged to the Pope to try to place his younger son Edmund on the disputed throne of the Island of Sicily down in the Mediterranean. As a result the king was seeking to pass measures through Parliament to raise funds from further taxation to help pay for his needs and a possible war.

But the barons were unhappy about this and led by Earl Simon they forced the king to accept a new form of constitutional government laid out in the Provisions of Oxford. These effectively went farther beyond Magna Carta in forcing kings to govern in consultation with their subjects.

Thus the Provisions of Oxford placed the king under the authority of a Council of fifteen members who were empowered to supervise ministerial appointments, national administration and the custody of royal castles.

Great Councils, which by now were being called Parliaments, were to meet three times a year and would monitor the performance of the Council of Fifteen.

Members of this Council of Fifteen included the great magnates such as Simon de Montfort and the Earls of Norfolk, Gloucester, Hereford and Warwick; also the Archbishops of Canterbury and Worcester plus the baron Roger de Mortimer. All supporters of these new reforms to certain conflicting extents.

Yet the changes brought about by the Oxford Parliament, also known as the 'Mad Parliament', did not however last for long without disputes developing.

Chapter 13 – 1259 to 1260

Margot sometimes travelled with Eleanor de Montfort and the extended family; she got to know the many sons of Simon and Eleanor – the eldest Henry; the slightly silly second son Simon The Younger; serious Amaury; and the easily led fourth son Guy.

She was pleased to be able to see Jean several times but he was often away on military tasks for Earl Simon.

When back in Gloucester, Margot also sometimes noticed a dark-haired man watching her – she now knew him to be Gilles de Bouton, a knight from Gloucester Castle and associated with the Earl of Gloucester and a follower of Simon de Montfort.

One day Margot was out walking in the midst of the crowded local market when a man bumped into her; Margot didn't notice anything untoward but when she went to pay for some lacework she found that her purse was cut and missing.

However just then a dirty, thin young boy came up to her and held out her purse to her saying "I saw a man stealing this from you, and as you are such a pretty young lady I thought I would get it back to return to you, mistress."

"So you lifted it back off him then?" replied a smiling Margot.

"Yes, he is not as clever as he thinks" laughed the boy.

"What is your name then?"

"It is Tom, Tom Buckle; and I move about a bit and live on the streets as best I can" he said.

"Well Tom, you look like you could do with a good meal. As you have done me a good service it is the least I can provide you with."

And so Tom followed Margot to her home and she ordered the cook to put a platter of cold meats and bread and ale before the boy.

The boy ravenously tore into the food and devoured it.

He sat back and noisily burped "Lovely food, mistress, and right good thanks to you."

"What will you do now, young Tom?" thoughtfully asked Margot.

"Dunno, probably best to move on soon to somewhere like Worcester to avoid any trouble."

"Tell you what – would you like to stay here for a bit longer – I could use a boy to undertake some important tasks and take messages for me – would you like to do that and work for me?"

"Why mistress that would be lovely!"

"There would be a pallet bed and good food for you to eat."

"A bed and food – I like the idea of all that" he laughed out.

"Well it is settled then, you shall live here and work for me – and it will not be too much hard work. But first I think you need a good bath!"

So Margot summoned her maidservant and got her to bring some soap and hot water from the kitchen to fill a small metal hipbath for the boy to wash in out in the yard.

Presently the young boy came back in looking surprisingly clean and fresh-looking in some ill-fitting clothes borrowed off the cook's younger brother.

"My, my, you have scrubbed up well" smiled Margot "and tomorrow we will get you some better clothes of your own to wear."

"Thank you mistress, much appreciated."

And so young Tom joined Margot's household and proved most useful in running errands and soon became friendly with old Gwyn the Innkeeper too.

Tom was very attached to Margot and most concerned about her safety, so would often accompany her when she went out or sometimes quietly shadow her movements in the background.

And Margot liked the cheerful company of the boy and found him helpful and reliable.

Chapter 14 – 1260 to 1261

King Henry had already made peace with King Louis IX of France in the December 1259 Treaty of Paris whereby Henry relinquished his claims to Normandy and certain other French lands, but Louis allowed him to keep Aquitaine and Gascony though only as a vassal to the King of France.

Finally in 1261 the Pope excused King Henry of his obligations related to trying to rage war for the throne of Sicily, and thus he no longer required the funds he was trying to get through Parliament from additional taxation.

So Henry set about reasserting his control of government. The baronial opposition responded but then backed down and Richard de Clare, Earl of Gloucester, more conservative in his demands for royal reform switched over to the king's side.

As his support waned, Simon de Montfort and his family again left England for France.

Chapter 15 – 1262 to 1263

Margot kept up her information gathering and regularly met up with Gwyn the Innkeeper, who she believed was in contact with the Welsh Princes. All this while Jean was away in France with Earl Simon.

Trouble rumbled on as the king's policy failures and the renewal of provocative and restrictive acts against the power of the barons inflamed hostility once more.

Then in July 1262 Henry's chief enforcer Richard de Clare died and his nearly nineteen year old son Gilbert became the 7th Earl of Gloucester and 6th Earl of Hertford.

Earl Richards's death weakened the position of the king especially as his impetuous young son now sided with the radical baronial opposition.

In April 1263 Simon de Montfort decided to return to England, and finally Margot could get to see Jean again when he returned to Gloucester Castle to meet up with the new young Earl Gilbert.

"It is good to see you once again Margot. My, you have grown even more beautiful since I last saw you" said Jean with a smile.

"You flatter me, kind sir" mocked Margot back, "I am surprised you even remember me it is so long ago!"

"I could never forget you" he shyly replied with a wistful look.

Margot introduced Jean to young Tom and explained how useful he had become as a good servant and messenger for her.

Tom looked on with some slight jealousy as he did not wish to share Mistress Margot with anyone else new.

But Jean tried to put him at ease and said he was sure they would both get along and work together to keep Margot safe.

Now that was something that Tom could agree upon!

Chapter 16 – 1263 to 1264

In the meantime Earl Simon gathered together a council of dissident barons at Oxford.

Fighting between the opposing parties broke out and by the autumn both sides had raised considerable armies.

Simon de Montfort eventually marched on London and the people of the city rose up in revolt, trapping the king and queen within the confines of the Tower of London.

They were taken prisoner and Earl Simon assumed effective control of government using King Henry's name.

However Simon's support soon fractured and King Henry was able to regain his liberty.

With violent disorder spreading and the prospect of all-out civil war looming Henry appealed to the auspices of King Louis IX of France for arbitration.

After initial resistance to what he saw as a time-wasting ploy, a hard-pressed Simon de Montfort consented to this hoping for restoration of the Provisions of Oxford.

Whilst all this was happening, Jean and Margot resolved to try and make direct contact with Prince Edward to make him aware of the assistance they were offering.

Jean heard that he was going to be in Hereford in a few days time and so Margot accompanied by Tom rode off from Gloucester to go there.

After making good speed on the journey, Margot presented herself at the castle with an intriguing letter written tantalisingly for the Prince alone to read.

His interest piqued, Prince Edward called for her to be brought to him and Margot curtseyed deeply and told him about her loyalty and desire for royal victory over Simon de Montfort.

She was impressed by his great height and bold vigour, and said that she and her confederates were well placed to spy for him and would do anything they could to aid him and the king.

In turn Prince Edward was charmed and captivated by the pledges of this earnest and attractive young woman and realised he could always do with more good intelligence information.

So giving her a small bag of coins, he urged her to carry on her clandestine work and keep him informed of any urgent and vital news.

The next day as Margot and Tom rode back into Gloucester they were watched by a thoughtful Gilles de Bouton, who considered precisely from which direction they were returning.

Chapter 17 – January to Easter 1264

Simon de Montfort was prevented from presenting the barons' case directly to King Louis due to a broken leg, but little suspected that the King of France, long known for his innate sense of justice, would so one-sidedly decide in favour of King Henry.

The Mise of Amiens settlement given out in January 1264 was firmly in favour of the royal prerogative and completely annulled the terms of the Provisions of Oxford.

This did little to dampen the smouldering conflict and the outcome was unacceptable to the more rebellious barons who prepared to resist any reassertion of strict royal power.

Both sides gathered their forces for the resumption of fighting which occurred in February 1264 with rebel attacks on royalist supporters in the Welsh Marches border region.

Now also another foul and odious turn of events happened.

A major part of Simon de Montfort's further appeal to the other barons was the call for cancellation of all debts owed to Jews.

A series of horrible attacks on Jewish communities followed involving massacres of Jews by his supporters in order to obtain and destroy the financial records which held details of the loans given out.

The attack and killings in Worcester in February 1264 were led by Earl Simon's own eldest son Henry and Robert Earl Ferrers.

At Easter 1264 in London one of Simon's key followers led the heinous attack in which up to 500 Jews died in the chaos; and this John Fitz John is said to have killed leading Jewish figures Isaac fil Aaron and Cok fil Abraham with his bare hands.

There were further abhorrent attacks on Jewish communities in Winchester, Canterbury, Lincoln and other towns.

Simply put the Second Barons' War was being fought over money and power and who had control.

All the while a lot of manoeuvring of the opposing armies carried on as both sides tried to gain an advantage.

Chapter 18 – May 1264

Fighting spread from London into Kent and then moved into Sussex. In May 1264 the king's army reached the town of Lewes where they intended to halt to allow further reinforcements to reach them.

King Henry encamped at St. Pancras Priory with the infantry, whilst Prince Edward commanded the cavalry housed at the nearby Lewes Castle.

Simon de Montfort approached Henry with the intention of either negotiating a truce or failing that to draw him into battle.

The king rejected the negotiations brusquely, whilst Earl Simon moved his men in a night march that surprised the royalist forces to Offham Hill, high ground a mile to the North West of Lewes.

The king's army was nearly twice the size of the rebels – King Henry held command of the centre; Prince Edward was on the right with the Earl of Pembroke and the Earl of Surrey; Henry's brother Richard of Cornwall and his son Henry of Almain were on the left.

Simon de Montfort split his forces into four parts – giving his eldest son Henry de Montfort command of one quarter; Gilbert de Clare and John Fitz John another quarter; a third portion consisting of Londoners placed under Nicholas de Segrave; whilst Earl Simon himself led the fourth quarter. His men were ordered to wear white crosses as a distinguishing emblem.

The baronial forces commenced the battle on 14th May 1264 with a surprise dawn attack on foragers sent out from the royal camp. King Henry's men then responded and Prince Edward led a swift cavalry charge.

Earl Simon had broken his leg in a riding accident several months earlier and still discomforted often travelled in a covered carriage.

When fighting began and Prince Edward's cavalry charge broke through he then charged towards the carriage; when he reached it and opened the door Edward was infuriated to find Earl Simon not in there!

Edward and his men carried on and then assaulted the London contingent placed on the left of the baronial line, which caused them to break and flee towards the village of Offham.

Prince Edward's cavalry wildly pursued his routed foes for some four miles, but thus leaving the king unsupported and vulnerable.

King Henry then decided to launch an attack with his infantry straight up Offham Hill into the main baronial line which awaited them at the defensive up on the higher ground.

Cornwall's division faltered almost immediately but Henry's men fought on well until compelled to retreat by the arrival of Simon de Montfort's men that had been held in reserve.

The king's soldiers were then forced further back down the hill and into the town of Lewes itself where they engaged in a fighting retreat towards the castle and Priory.

Prince Edward finally returned with his weary cavalrymen and launched a counterattack. But upon locating his father in the Priory he was persuaded that with the town ablaze and many of the king's supporters having fled, it was time to accept de Montfort's offer of terms and surrender.

The Earl of Cornwall was captured by the barons' men when he was unable to reach the safety of the Priory, and being discovered in a windmill he was taunted with raucous cries of "Come down, come down, thou worst of millers!"

After his capitulation, the king was made to sign the Mise of Lewes which forced him to accept the terms of the Provisions of Oxford again.

Prince Edward was made a hostage of the barons and although not imprisoned as such was kept in close confinement under guard.

But the prince vowed to reverse the humiliation of this defeat and redress the mistakes that had led to the royal downfall.

This victory put Simon de Montfort in a position of supreme power and made him almost the 'uncrowned King of England'.

And shortly thereafter Earl Simon announced the cancellation of all debts owed to the Jews, as he had made a large part of his promises to the other barons.

Chapter 19 – June 1264 to March 1265

This was the high-water mark of Simon de Montfort's success. The radicalism of de Montfort's subversion of the traditional order was once again to lead to a fracturing of his brittle base of support.

Most of the barons had originally been against the bad government, favouritism and wastefulness of the king; but now they found it went against the grain to see one of their own number in a position to forcefully dictate to them.

And he attracted criticism from many of the barons for excluding others from power and handing castles, money and offices to his sons and friends.

This was all bubbling away under the surface as Earl Simon used his victory to set up a government based on the 1258 Provisions of Oxford leaving the king as little more than a figurehead.

There can however be no doubt that the common man was for Earl Simon but they did not have much money nor wield much power.

Simon de Montfort successfully held a parliament in London in June 1264 to confirm new constitutional arrangements in England.

But he was unable to properly consolidate his victory at Lewes and widespread disorder persisted across the country.

In France Queen Eleanor made plans for an invasion of England with the support of King Louis.

In response, and hoping to win wider support for his government, Simon de Montfort summoned a new Parliament for January 1265. He sent for not only the barons, senior churchmen and two knights from each county, but also two burgesses or representatives from each of the major towns such as York, Lincoln and the Cinque Ports which was the first time this had been done.

But due to a growing lack of support among the barons, only twenty-three of them turned up in comparison to the summons issued to 120 churchmen, who largely supported the new government.

The Great Parliament as it became known as was nominally overseen by King Henry and was held in the Palace of Westminster just outside the city of London, whose continuing loyalty was essential to de Montfort's cause.

It is called the Great Parliament not because of what it actually accomplished but on account of the precedent it set. It is often referred to as the first representative English Parliament including lords, churchmen and commoners.

But it was also a populist, tactical move by Earl Simon in an attempt to gather support from the regions and it was a very partisan assembly, not perhaps with any grand ideas of a true display of democratic establishment.

However it did set a precedent and unlock the door for the future direction of parliamentary government.

Finally in early March 1265, both King Henry and Prince Edward were required to swear again to abide by the Magna Carta and the Provisions of Oxford.

Prince Edward was to have his liberty as such again, but he had to continue under restrictions for three years and not consort with foreigners and others to disrupt the realm.

He was delivered into the custody of his father but yet still under the overall control of de Montfort's followers.

This Great Parliament brought some temporary calm but then opposition grew once more, particularly as it was further seen that Simon de Montfort and his immediate family began to amass huge power and fortune.

Chapter 20 – April to May 1265

Prince Edward was often in the company of Simon's eldest son Henry de Montfort, and as Margot knew him well from her dealings with his mother and the whole family she took the opportunity to visit Henry.

And whilst there and using the pretext of this visit she was secretly able to pass word onto Prince Edward that his friends of the Seven Knights from the Welsh Marches were planning to hopefully soon release him from the close confines of his situation.

When later on back in Gloucester, Margot also went up to the castle and saw Gilbert de Clare who was chaffing at the lack of preferment he was being given by Earl Simon.

In fact the impetuous young man was full of anger and rage at his apparent hard-done-to situation – he was ripe for cajoling and persuading that in fact he might be better off now considering supporting the royalist cause.

Margot sweetly dripped in his ear the idea of how much better appreciated he would be by a restored king and his vital young son the Prince Edward.

After Margot had left a watchful Gilles de Bouton, who was a staunch follower of the radical reformers, could see that the young Earl of Gloucester had been swayed to a new course.

Gilles absented himself as he heard the young Earl call for horses to be brought and for his men to be roused to action.

Gilles went after the departing Margot and was keeping an eye on her when he sensed and then realised that he himself was also being followed.

Carefully at a corner he espied that it was a thin young boy tracking him from the shadows. It was Margot's servant lad Tom.

Just after he saw Margot near to reaching her house, Gilles swiftly doubled back behind the urchin and catching him unawares gave him a hard clout with his fist rendering the boy slightly senseless.

Gilles dragged him upright and clamping his hand over Tom's mouth to stop him from shouting out pulled him away back off towards the castle.

The groggy youngster was sullen but kept quiet when Gilles told him he would hit him again if he said anything at all.

On his return he avoided the Earl and his retainers who were just getting ready to leave, and Gilles took Tom to the corner tower in which the castle's dark dungeons were housed.

He told the dirty old jailer to lock the boy up and await his return. Then Gilles watched as Gilbert and his men rode out and next he went up to the Great Hall to get a cup of wine and think about what information he was going to try and force out of Tom.

Chapter 21 – May 1265

Margot got back home and found Jean there waiting for her. She told him how Gilbert de Clare was even now riding off to join up with royalist forces under the command of the Seven Knights led by Roger de Mortimer and Roger de Leyburn.

Jean informed her that events were turning against Earl Simon and he was attempting to get all his forces together to put an army back into the field.

Margot then asked her young maidservant where Tom was and the girl said that he had gone out earlier saying he was going to follow his mistress to keep an eye on her.

Margot was instantly worried and wondered where he was and what could have happened to him.

She and Jean went to see Gwyn at his inn and heard from him that some customer of his had said he had seen a young boy being forcibly frog-marched towards the castle by a tall dark dressed knight.

They realised it was Gilles de Bouton and that he had captured Tom, and he could even now be down in the dungeons beating him up and trying to get information out of him.

Jean and Margot resolved to try and set Tom free somehow. They decided a bold approach was needed and that Jean would deal with Gilles and keep him talking and occupied, whilst Margot tried to inveigle her way into the corner tower where the dungeons were below.

Jean set out to go up to the castle and Margot put on a thick dress under which she hid a sharp dagger, which she very much hoped she would not have to use later on.

Chapter 22 – May 1265

So in the late afternoon Margot walked up to the main gatehouse and requested to speak to the Earl of Gloucester again. The guards obviously told her that he was not there and asked what she wanted.

With trepidation Margot pulled out a copy of the seal of Simon de Montfort and said "I have come to see that young boy you are holding here. We believe he may be one of our servants who stole some valuables from us and then ran off. I have been sent to see if it is him by the Earl."

"Well I was told there were to be no visitors allowed" said the sergeant of the guards.

"Do you want to upset the Earl of Leicester?" icily replied Margot; "I am sure he would be most displeased. I demand to see the boy."

"Oh well, I suppose so. I don't want to upset the Earl and anyway you're only a woman after all."

So the guards took her inside and as they crossed the courtyard Margot could see the unguarded rear postern gate she had been told about.

She was escorted to the big corner tower and left in the jailer's anteroom.

"Well, well, well, my pretty; what you be doing here visiting old Jake then?" said the gnarled old lummox of a jailer.

"I have heard tell of that boy who was locked up and wanted to see him."

"Why be that then?" suspiciously asked the old man.

"Because my master wondered if it was our servant boy who stole some things from us and ran away. I should like to see if it is him or not."

"And what you be giving old Jake to let you see him?" leered the grubby little jailer.

"I will give you a couple of coins – that should suffice."

"What about a little kiss as well then?"

"I don't think your castle warden would be pleased to hear of such impertinence to the Earl's trusted servant!"

"All right now, hold your horses; I'll let you see him. Where's those coins you were mentioning?"

Margot handed over two small silver pennies and the jailer then led her down some wet stone steps into the slimy and dank dungeons at the very bottom of the tower.

Several heavy, old wooden doors showed the various cells down there.

Margot fretted and wondered how she was going to overpower the jailer and get Tom out. Surreptitiously she picked up a small wooden stool lying over to one side.

Old Jake shambled over to the cell on the right and after fumbling with a bunch of keys opened the heavy door and pushed it inwards.

Chapter 23 – May 1265

From the light of a spluttering torch hanging up outside, Margot could just see young Tom who was bruised and bloody after obviously having been beaten up.

Tom looked up and seeing Margot smiled and half-raised himself slightly; Margot shook her head slowly motioning him to quieten.

Old Jake grumbled "Well is this your runaway servant boy then?"

"I can't be sure; can you move the door further so the light shines in more?"

And as he did that Margot hit him hard with the wooden stool she had picked up and knocked him unconscious.

She rushed into the gloomy cell and went over to Tom and using the jailer's keys managed to unlock him from his shackles.

"Oh mistress, you came to save me!"

"You should have known I would not simply leave you to rot in this grim dungeon."

"But you have risked everything to get me out."

"Well we've not escaped yet. We have to get out of this tower and then across the courtyard and out through the rear gate."

They dragged the unconscious jailer into the cell and locked him in with his own keys, which they kept hold of as they would need them later.

"I hope he doesn't die, mistress, or your eternal soul will be put in peril. He wasn't one of them that hit me you know."

"I am sure he will wake up later with a bad headache and he may even be in quite a bit of trouble. I hit him hard but I had to make sure the vile man went down. If he keeps quiet about them he may still have those silver pennies to spend."

"Fraid not mistress, I picked them up off him on our way out!"

Tom was feeling fairly sore and shaky and Margot had to get him to put an arm around her shoulders to help him move along.

They walked up the stone steps and into the jailer's anteroom. Night was falling as Margot looked out of the window and seeing that the courtyard was clear she helped Tom to hobble over to the outside door.

The door was locked and Margot frantically tried all the keys on the jailer's metal ring but none of them seemed to work and the door remained locked.

Margot started to panic as she realised that they might be stuck there unable to get out and waiting to be discovered when the jailer was missed. She took a deep breath and tried all the keys again more slowly; finally one of them turned in the lock and released the door.

Much relieved Margot and Tom opened the door a chink and looking across the empty courtyard they slipped out.

Now was the time to cast no shadow as they walked around the corner tower trying to avoid the light from the flickering torches hanging from iron brackets on the dark stone walls.

The rear postern gate was slightly ajar and they pushed through it.

Outside slumped grotesquely on the ground was the body of Gilles de Bouton lying dead in a spreading pool of blood.

In the darkening gloom Margot could just make out the shadow of a departing figure limping away in the distance. Surely it must be Jean and what exactly had been happening out here?

Feeling chilled but glad to be out they unsteadily walked back towards home.

Chapter 24 – May 1265

When Margot walked back into her parlour she propped Tom up in a chair, and then found Jean sitting on a bench with his bloody hand clasped to his left side.

Margot let out a gasp and ran over to him – Jean winced in pain and said "I'll be all right; it looks worse than it is."

"It looks quite bad to me. What happened? I thought you were just going to keep Gilles occupied and out of the way."

"I tried to, but I could sense that he didn't trust me and I think he guessed that something wasn't quite right about you and me and everything."

"He was always keeping an eye on the mistress" piped up Tom.

Margot realised she had two men to look after and called for her maidservant to bring hot water and bandages to clean and patch up their bodies and strong brandywine to fortify their spirits. After being bandaged up Jean took a long drink and sighed as he started to tell the whole tale.

"Gilles was acting rather strange and then he said he had to go and check if the postern gate was properly locked and would I come with him. When we got out there he fiddled with the keys and then came at me with a knife."

"He caught me with a slash to my left side but I managed to beat him off, and we fought and tussled and rolled about and I turned his own knife on him and he died."

"Fortunately there was no one else about; I unlocked the gate and dragged him outside and then left it open hopefully for you to get out through."

"Thank goodness you left it open for us or we would never have got out of there."

"What are we going to do now?" said Jean.

"Gilbert de Clare is on his way westwards to join up with the Seven Knights and they have a plan to spring Prince Edward from his close confinement."

"What can we do next then?"

"Well you and Tom are going to have to stay here lying low unseen to mend your wounds and get better. I will ask Gwyn to keep an eye out for you."

"However there is something I can do; I shall go to London and try and delay Simon The Younger. He is foolish and susceptible and I am sure I can hold him up when his father would rather like him to be on the move with his forces."

So leaving them there grumbling about her going away, Margot hired a good horse and hitching up her skirts set out for London.

Chapter 25 – May 1265

Troubles seemed to multiply for Earl Simon. He heard that Gilbert de Clare had left Gloucester and moved westwards and had a considerable force of armed men with him.

It was now also being rumoured that he was in communication with Mortimer and Leyburn, the royalist ringleaders of the Seven Knights.

Determined to get to the bottom of the situation, Simon de Montfort went to Gloucester, also taking the king with him, to arrange a meeting with young Earl Gilbert.

The Earl of Gloucester came back but would not come into the town, but instead camped just outside the walls with his men. The light of his campfires lit up the night sky showing the large force he had come with.

Negotiations were conducted but they proved not very satisfactory to either side.

Gilbert de Clare was still upset over the amount of power Simon and his family had and what he believed was an unfair division of the spoils of victory, despite the fact that he had received quite a lot.

Simon de Montfort felt he could not trust Earl Gilbert anymore and that he certainly could not be depended upon for his help in any future fighting.

Then Earl Simon heard that William of Valence and the Earl of Surrey, prominent escapees from the Battle of Lewes who had previously made it over to exile in France, had returned and landed at Pembroke in Wales with the intention of joining other royalist forces in renewing the struggle.

Chapter 26 – May 1265

Next a truly pivotal event occurred.

Prince Edward was nominally under the custody of his father the king, but a close watch and tight control on his movements was being exercised.

However he was desperate to escape from his confinement and take up the fight again.

Staying at that time at Hereford Castle he knew that not very far away were some of his former close companions from the Welsh Marches.

Maud de Mortimer, the wife of Roger, based at nearby Wigmore Castle devised an ingenious plan of how to organise his escape and the details were passed onto him.

On 28th May 1265 Prince Edward spent the whole day out in the open hunting with companions including Henry de Montfort who were charged with keeping an eye on him.

They had ridden out from Hereford Castle and also proceeded to race their horses in lighthearted competition. Edward took part in the fun riding several horses at different points.

Finally he mounted a fine stallion which through clever manipulation had not yet been used in any of the racing.

Riding casually on his fresh mount Prince Edward managed to draw free of his close companions without rousing any great suspicion in the minds of those accompanying him.

Suddenly at this point a lone horseman appeared in the distance and raised an arm in salute. This was the signal the prince had been waiting for and he spurred his horse and made off at top speed.

The others on their partly winded horses could not catch up with him and they fell back and looked on helplessly as

Prince Edward joined up with a group of horsemen who emerged to take him off.

They made for Wigmore Castle some twenty miles away, where later the waiting chatelaine Maud de Mortimer was able to welcome the prince.

Changing horses at Wigmore, Prince Edward then rode on to Ludlow Castle a further ten miles away where he met up with Maud's husband Roger and also Gilbert de Clare who agreed to transfer his allegiance.

Edward was pleased to now have the support of the powerful Earl of Gloucester and made plans to renew the conflict and beat Simon de Montfort and the rebel barons.

This daring escape also galvanised support for the royal cause in the West and further weakened the rebels.

And Prince Edward also rapidly began using offers of royal patronage and bribes to help sway and win over many of the less radical barons.

Chapter 27 – June 1265

Earl Simon was naturally dismayed by the speed with which events had turned against him. He had hoped and expected that peace would have followed the pronouncements of the Great Parliament and the king had seemed acquiescent to the whole situation.

Simon de Montfort was getting old and must have been feeling tired and weary; but he was a man of action and he boldly made moves to bolster his fortunes.

Simon roused his men and got ready to leave his dear wife for yet another time.

"Once more I must leave you to try and sort out this unholy mess."

"The cause of liberty and justice puts a heavy burden on you, my husband" said Eleanor.

"It is a weight I would gladly bear to try and make this a better and more just land" he replied.

The Lady Eleanor turned away, tears pricking her eyes.

Earl Simon gently twisted her around and embraced her.

"Afraid, alas, and why so suddenly."

"Oh, my dear husband, I am afraid and I do not want to lose you."

"Ah, mine heart, remember me well."

The Earl gave her one last kiss and strode out through the door.

Through her tears his wife Eleanor mumbled "Jesu, mercy, how may this be?"

Swiftly he marched into Southern Wales and made a deal with Llywelyn ap Gruffudd, Prince of Wales, which maybe bore the signs of desperation including betrothing his youngest daughter Eleanor, then aged just thirteen to the older man for marriage at a later date.

In return Llywelyn offered the promise of money in the future and also provided some military assistance now in the form of a small body of several hundred Welsh archers.

Next Earl Simon sent instructions to his second son, Simon The Younger, to gather what forces he could in London and the South and East and then march with all haste to join up with his father.

Simon de Montfort then moved South along the western bank of the River Severn to try and cross over and attack Bristol.

But he was unfortunately unable to find unguarded places and ways to get across, and so he turned around and marched back up the western bank of the river towards Hereford.

Earl Simon really needed his son Simon The Younger to turn up with the much required reinforcements from London and the South and East.

No good could possibly come of their cause without these extra men joining up to increase their numbers to match those of the growing royal army.

Chapter 28 – July 1265

But unfortunately for Simon de Montfort's cause his second son at this point was still a very great distance away and moving with major hesitation and indecisiveness.

Simon The Younger had allowed himself to be delayed in London and a major reason was his dallying with a beautiful young lady – Margot!

Margot had travelled to London and insinuated herself into Simon's company and kept him much preoccupied with her when he should have been rushing to get his troops prepared.

Simon The Younger had said "I have always desired you, Margot, ever since I first saw you and have wanted you like this."

"Well now you may take your pleasure" coquettishly smiled Margot.

But if Simon had his way with her, it was Margot that was allowing the seduction in order to tangle him up and scramble his thinking.

Simon The Younger dallied with Margot for much longer than he should have. He delayed in London when he should have already been on the road to seek to join up with his father's forces.

Belatedly he set out with his men and headed up towards Kenilworth Castle, the Midlands stronghold of the de Montforts.

Margot accompanied them and kept young Simon suitably distracted as they finally reached the great red brick built castle.

Chapter 29 – July 1265

Simon The Younger, feeling safe and secure in his location and far away from any potential enemy, had not thought it necessary to bring his men inside the vast impregnable walls of Kenilworth Castle.

He had left them out in the open, with some billeted in the nearby town and many in tents in the fields around the castle site.

Margot decided now was the perfect time to take this vital piece of information to Prince Edward.

She waited till mid-morning and then disguising herself as a man she slipped out to the horselines and took a fine horse to ride.

She easily rode away from the busy camp without any difficulty and made for Prince Edward's known current headquarters at Worcester more than thirty miles away.

After a hard journey Margot arrived at Worcester later in the afternoon; she was stopped by sentries and demanded to see Prince Edward with urgent news.

The soldiers looked askance at this mud-splattered horseman who fidgeted impatiently in front of them, but then Margot pulled off her cap and her long hair tumbled down.

The sentries gasped with astonishment and Margot told them to hurry up and take her to the prince. They called for the officer of the watch and he swiftly escorted her to the prince's headquarters tent.

When Margot was shown into the tent Prince Edward and his commanders looked up in surprise.

"Well my dear lady, what are you doing here in such a state?"

Margot curtseyed and replied "Your Highness, I come with news of great importance about your enemies. Simon the Younger has arrived at Kenilworth but all his men are encamped outside the castle."

Prince Edward smiled "Ah, that is indeed most interesting and welcome intelligence. I thank you for having ridden so hard with this vital information. Comrades let us see how we can turn this to our advantage."

Edward realised that his army was in the middle between Earl Simon in the West at Hereford and Simon The Younger in Warwickshire at Kenilworth.

The royal army was now at least equal to the whole size of the baronial forces; but if brought against just one part of his enemies he should have sufficient strength to defeat them individually.

Margot's intelligence made the choice of going and attacking Simon The Younger's ill-prepared forces of paramount importance.

Chapter 30 – July 1265

Prince Edward acted with great speed and marched his whole army out of Worcester.

They rapidly covered the distance of over thirty miles in somewhere around twelve or thirteen hours; arriving at Kenilworth just before dawn on the following day, the 31st July 1265.

Margot on a fresh horse came along with them, and as they reached the town she was sent to the rear to stay out of harm's way when fighting commenced.

Finding the army of Simon The Younger spread out and sleeping soundly either in town beds or under tent canvas, Prince Edward gave the order to attack.

Rather than a pitched battle it was a brutal surprise attack that resulted in the shattering and scattering of the baronial troops.

Some very perplexed leaders were caught completely unawares and taken prisoner.

All the army's horses were captured still in their horselines, and also many of their brightly-coloured military banners were taken from where they had been propped up in amongst the tents.

Many soldiers fled and ran away and scattered over the surrounding countryside – this time Prince Edward did not allow his men to go off and pursue the fugitives.

Some bewildered soldiers managed to swim across the moat and took refuge behind the walls of the castle.

Simon The Younger shamefacedly looked out on the scene of this terrible disaster with anger and frustration, and cursed his stupidity in not setting proper guards and making sensible preparations for his men's protection and safety.

Then he saw in the far distance a woman with long hair who he thought he maybe recognised – and he crushingly realised how Prince Edward had come to hear of his army's position.

"So, go faithless friend, I don't see you anymore as an angel of mercy!" he mouthed bitterly under his breath.

Chapter 31 – August 1265

With Simon The Younger's part of the baronial forces defeated and destroyed, Prince Edward gathered his troops together and without pause set off to go and deal with Earl Simon next.

Having all those captured horses helped and the spirits of the men were high as they realised that half of the victory had already been won and they were in the ascendancy.

So they rapidly proceeded South West back towards Worcester.

The Prince thanked Margot again for her vital information and gave her a large bag of gold coins and a pair of exquisite pearl earrings as gifts for her great loyalty to the royal cause. Then Margot headed off back to her home in Gloucester.

In the meantime with knowledge that Prince Edward's army was no longer then in Worcester (which was worrying in itself) Earl Simon finally had managed to get his tired army across the River Severn at Kempsey on 3rd August.

He was worried what was happening elsewhere, but was determined to try and join up with his second son's forces wherever they may be, presumably somewhere between London and Kenilworth.

Simon de Montfort marched onto the town of Evesham which lay in a loop of the River Avon and decided to stop there for the night.

Whilst Earl Simon was doing all that, Prince Edward and his men arrived back in Worcester after much hard marching also on 3rd August.

Straightaway his scouts told the prince that Earl Simon's army had been spotted and was even then heading for Evesham.

Prince Edward whooped with joyous delight at this news and roused his men for one final effort.

Grumbling perhaps, they fell into line again, and in the fading light began another night march East towards Alcester and then South down to Evesham.

A plan of battle was agreed on during the night and the army split into three parts.

Gilbert de Clare, the Earl of Gloucester, was to take his wing down the western arm of the River Avon to prevent Earl Simon from escaping West towards the River Severn.

Roger de Mortimer with his wing was detailed to cross the eastern arm of the loop of the River Avon and not only block the one bridge across the river there but also then seek to get behind the rebel army.

Prince Edward with the main bulk of the royal army would drive straight down against the baronial forces in Evesham.

The final battle of the conflict was about to be fought.

Chapter 32 – August 1265

Just around daybreak and the first appearance of light in the sky on 04th August 1265 Simon de Montfort's scouts noticed the approach of armed forces to the North of the town.

They were being led by paraded banners known to them and this initially convinced them into thinking that the armed men were the hoped-for reinforcements of Simon The Younger.

But as they continued to advance onwards then grim realisation hit home and they saw and understood that the enemy army was upon them.

Earl Simon's tired and weary force of around four to five thousand men was faced by a royal army of about double the size, namely roughly ten thousand strong.

Simon de Montfort still held King Henry III captive with him and had the king hastily dressed in armour and saddled up so as to have him accompany them in the battle.

However without any distinguishing shield or banner it was quite likely that the unidentified king could die under the blows of those royal soldiers who were fighting to free him!

Earl Simon's position was desperate and he fully realised it.

Yet he noted the sound dispositions of the prince's royal army up on the higher ground of Green Hill looking down on Evesham and Simon exclaimed "They have not learned that for themselves, but were taught it by me."

Then the hopelessness of the situation caused him to remark to those about him, including his sons Henry and Guy "May God have mercy on our souls, for our bodies are theirs!"

But he did not consider surrender and assembled his men for a bold charge. He decided to form his men into a wedge led by his heavily armed knights and attack up the hill concentrating on the centre of the prince's battle force.

Suddenly an ominous, big black cloud appeared over the royal army and a thunderstorm started to rage as the rebels advanced.

Chapter 33 – August 1265

The first clash of the battle lines occurred and the baronial wedge carried well into the royal line, but it held and did not break and then its extended wings bent and closed in around the sides of Earl Simon's men.

The Earl and his followers found themselves hemmed in with the impetus of their attack expended. They were fighting desperately for their lives now.

A dozen knights of the royal army had been designated to act as a death squad and were even now stalking the battlefield with orders to target and hunt down Simon de Montfort.

The battle rapidly turned against the rebels and quickly became a bloody massacre and slaughter.

Simon's son Guy was badly wounded and captured, and then his eldest son Henry was cut down before his eyes.

It is reported the brave Earl was heard to say "Now it is time for me to die" and shortly thereafter he was slain and the great leader of the barons' rebellion was no more.

But the war had generated so much bitter hatred that his dead body was terribly mutilated and hacked to pieces.

Roger de Mortimer, who had crossed the river to join in the fighting, is supposed to have been the ringleader of this horrible behaviour as the head, hands and feet were cut off.

Later the bloody head of Earl Simon was paraded high on the point of a lance and was then sent by Roger de Mortimer to his wife Maud at Wigmore Castle where it was displayed as a gruesome trophy.

Despite despairing attempts to surrender most of the baronial rebels were killed on the battlefield rather than taken prisoner and ransomed, as was often the common custom and practice.

"Such was the murder of Evesham, for battle it was not" wrote a contemporary chronicler.

Of the 160 knights who accompanied Earl Simon onto the field of battle only twelve survived; it was an episode of noble bloodletting unprecedented in those tumultuous times.

King Henry had been rescued unharmed early on in the battle and was now restored back to his kingly power.

The rebels were completely disinherited and their lands confiscated and taken into the king's hands to keep or distribute.

Prince Edward gave orders that what remained of the mutilated body of Earl Simon should be collected and buried at the nearby Evesham Abbey.

Then King Henry III and Prince Edward left the bloody place of battle and headed back to the capital of London.

And the cause of reform at that time was also buried along with Simon de Montfort's dead body.

Chapter 34 – August to September 1265

In the meantime Margot had returned to Gloucester and was welcomed by Jean and Tom who had both recovered from their wounds and ordeals.

She told them what she had done to pass on that vital intelligence information to Prince Edward and his subsequent great triumph at Kenilworth and of his generous reward.

But she did not tell them exactly everything she had done to enable her to bring her intrigue to fruition.

Soon after they heard the momentous news that Earl Simon had been defeated and killed at the Battle of Evesham.

When she heard that his body had been horribly mutilated, Margot felt a slight twinge of remorse for even though he had been behind so much wrong done to so many including her family and friends, she still remembered him as a bold and vigorous man.

Several weeks later Margot sold her house in Gloucester and they said a fond goodbye to Gwyn the Innkeeper as Margot and Jean accompanied by Tom Buckle left to head to a port on the South coast.

They were sailing over to France and then going back to Margot and Jean's old homeland of Gascony to get married and live.

They had enough gold and money to buy a fine house and land back where they had both come from.

And young Tom was happy to go wherever they were going – it was a fine end to their adventures and he was sure they were set fair for good times ahead.

Epilogue

In regard to wide-scale confrontations the Battle of Evesham proved decisive and left the royalists in a totally dominant position.

But some of the surviving rebels continued to defend their strongholds, most notably Kenilworth Castle, and the war dragged on.

In 1266 Simon The Younger and his remaining supporters were now stuck inside the thick walls of Kenilworth Castle.

Having initially promised to surrender the castle to King Henry, Simon The Younger later changed his mind and so the king decided to lay siege to the castle starting on 21st June 1266.

Kenilworth was a massive castle much surrounded by water and well provisioned and defended.

What followed was a siege that lasted six months, making it possibly the longest siege ever conducted on English soil.

King Henry was persuaded to seek some compromise agreement, and a commission of bishops and barons drafted a proclamation known as the Dictum of Kenilworth issued on 31st October 1266.

This set out terms under which the remaining rebels could secure a pardon and ultimately regain their confiscated lands, admittedly on payment of heavy fines.

The proposals were initially rejected by the rebels, but on 14th December 1266 hunger finally compelled the defenders of Kenilworth Castle to surrender, accepting the terms of the Dictum.

It was then discovered that the castle had only two days worth of food left remaining.

Simon The Younger and his younger brother Guy managed to escape from the castle and travelled to France and Italy where they found employment and fought as soldiers of fortune.

In March 1271 they discovered their royal cousin Henry of Almain, son of King Henry's brother Richard of Cornwall, was returning from the Crusades through Italy.

They found him taking Mass at a church in Viterbo and in front of the holy altar Simon and Guy brutally and viciously murdered him.

They were then both excommunicated from the Holy Church by the Pope for this heinous and blasphemous crime.

Later on that year Simon The Younger died from Toscana Virus contracted from the bite of an infected sandfly, deemed "Cursed by God, a wanderer and a fugitive."

The death of King Henry III in 1272 led to the accession of his son as King Edward I and the kingdom now entered into a period of unity and relative progress that lasted into the early 1290's.

Gradually however King Edward I was drawn towards military action and warfare, and he became known as the harsh conqueror of Wales and then subsequently as the Hammer of the Scots.

Furthermore in 1275 he issued the Statute of the Jewry that once more persecuted the Jewish population of England and imposed severe taxation on them.

Proving both lucrative and popular, Edward extended this policy of persecution and later on in 1279 leading Jews were arrested and many executed.

Finally in 1290 by the Edict of Expulsion all Jews were formally expelled from England, but without their remaining money and property which was forfeited to the Crown.

ALSO BY THIS AUTHOR...

FOR HONOUR AND NOT FOR GLORY

A young Briton, Drustan gets caught up in conflict in Britain including the AD43 Roman Invasion and ultimately the savage AD60/61 Revolt of Queen Boudica.

He encounters challenges to his honour but will not be defeated and throughout adversity he will continue to fight "For Honour And Not For Glory".

This short novelette offers up an exciting story linked to the legend of the Hallaton Helmet and hoard discovered in Leicestershire in 2000, now on display at the Market Harborough Museum.

£5.99   ISBN: 978-0-9567753-4-4

ALSO BY THIS AUTHOR...

ALL SINS MUST BE PAID FOR

Archaeologists working on the route of the Weymouth Relief Road in Dorset in 2008/2009 discovered a burial pit on Ridgeway Hill containing what turned out to be 54 dismembered skeletons and 51 skulls of Vikings executed by local Saxons.

This novelette seeks to offer a plausible tale of what could have happened at a time of great conflict in England between the Saxons under King Aethelred the Unready and the Danes led by Sweyn Forkbeard around the years AD 1002 to 1014.

It is told through the actions of Rolf, an innocent young boy who stows away on a longship heading across to England. But as the story unfolds, Rolf is drawn into a maelstrom of violence and death, and a burning need for revenge that is so all consuming that it changes him forever. And sometimes a man has to pay a heavy price to atone for all his misdeeds. But is there still a chance for redemption?

£5.99   ISBN: 978-0-9567753-5-1

ALSO BY THIS AUTHOR...

AWFUL THE MANY FOUL DEEDS

Rory and his younger sister Eva are
orphaned in Ireland and are taken in
by the kind Lady Affreca, the wife of
the English ruler of much of Ulster, the
famed and powerful knight John de Courcy.

But times are changing with the accession
of King John, a cruel and vindictive despot
who cares nothing for his subjects and the
rule of law. His dangerous spitefulness
will cause the downfall of many.

This short novelette goes back and forth
between Ireland and Wales in the early
1200's as Rory is forced to go on the run to
keep one step ahead of royal displeasure.
Along the way there are friends and foes to
deal with in a search for some peace and safety.

£5.99   ISBN: 978-0-9567753-7-5

David's 30 Favourite Rock & Pop Albums

1964	(01)	The Beatles	A Hard Day's Night
1976	(02)	Be-Bop Deluxe	Sunburst Finish
1971	(03)	Caravan	In The Land Of Grey And Pink
1979	(04)	Ry Cooder	Bop Till You Drop
1991	(05)	Crowded House	Woodface
1972	(06)	Deep Purple	Machine Head
1978	(07)	Dire Straits	Dire Straits
1975	(08)	Eagles	One Of These Nights
1977	(09)	Fleetwood Mac	Rumours
1970	(10)	Free	Fire And Water
1973	(11)	Rory Gallagher	Tattoo
1973	(12)	Genesis	Selling England By The Pound
1968	(13)	Jimi Hendrix	Electric Ladyland
1971	(14)	Led Zeppelin	IV (Four Symbols)
1974	(15)	Little Feat	Feats Don't Fail Me Now
1973	(16)	Lynyrd Skynyrd	Pronounced Leh-nerd Skin-nerd
1973	(17)	Pink Floyd	Dark Side Of The Moon
1975	(18)	Pink Floyd	Wish You Were Here
1972	(19)	Steely Dan	Can't Buy A Thrill
1976	(20)	Steely Dan	The Royal Scam
1976	(21)	Al Stewart	Year Of The Cat
1971	(22)	Rod Stewart	Every Picture Tells A Story
1975	(23)	10CC	How Dare You!
1971	(24)	James Taylor	Mud Slide Slim And The Blue Horizon
1994	(25)	Martin Taylor	Spirit Of Django
2005	(26)	Thunder	The Magnificent Seventh
2001	(27)	Peter White	Glow
1971	(28)	The Who	Who's Next
1972	(29)	Wishbone Ash	Argus
1986	(30)	XTC	Skylarking

David's 20 Favourite Guitarists from his Youth

b.1910	DJANGO REINHARDT	Gypsy Jazz Guitarist
b.1933	JULIAN BREAM	Classical Guitarist and Lutenist
b.1942	JIMI HENDRIX	of JIMI HENDRIX EXPERIENCE
b.1944	JIMMY PAGE	of LED ZEPPELIN
b.1945	RITCHIE BLACKMORE	of DEEP PURPLE and RAINBOW
b.1945	DANNY GATTON	Rockabilly and Redneck Jazz
b.1946	PETER GREEN	of original FLEETWOOD MAC
b.1948	RORY GALLAGHER	Irish Blues Rock Guitarist
b.1948	BILL NELSON	of BE-BOP DELUXE
b.1949	ANDREW LATIMER	of CAMEL
b.1950	ANDY POWELL	of WISHBONE ASH
b.1950	TED TURNER	of WISHBONE ASH
b.1950	PAUL KOSSOFF	of FREE
b.1951	PETER HAYCOCK	of CLIMAX BLUES BAND
b.1951	WALTER TROUT	Blues Rock Guitarist
b.1951	ROBBEN FORD	Blues, Jazz and Rock Guitarist
b.1952	GARY MOORE	Rock and Blues Guitarist
b.1953	LAURIE WISEFIELD	of WISHBONE ASH
b.1954	STEVIE RAY VAUGHAN	"SRV" Blues Rock Guitarist
b.1956	MARTIN TAYLOR	Jazz and Solo Guitarist